HAYLEY BRIANA

Hearts of Resin

HEARTS OF RESIN

A Dark Stalker Romance

Hayley Briana

Copyright © 2024 by Hayley Briana

All rights reserved. No part of this publication may be reproduced, stored or transmitted in any form or by any means, electronic, mechanical, photocopying, recording, scanning, or otherwise, without written permission from the publisher. It is illegal to copy this book, post it to a website, or distribute it by any other means without permission.

<u>DON'T BE A DICK WHO STEALS FROM AUTHORS!</u>

This novel is entirely a work of fiction. The names, characters, and incidents portrayed in it are the work of the author's imagination. Any resemblance to actual persons, living or dead, events or localities is entirely coincidental.

Hayley asserts the moral right to be identified as the author of this work.

1st Edition

Formatting, cover design, interior artwork, and editing by Angel & Rose Publishing-Services

For the gals who love a stalker in a mask that likes to send you the hearts of those who hurt you wrapped in a box with a pretty bow

DISCLAIMER

This book contains explicit content and dark themes
that may be considered traumatic and offensive to some readers.
Please check triggers before reading.
If you are not comfortable with some of these topics, please put
this book down and do not read it.
This work is only for those 18 or older.

The relationship depicted in this book is toxic and is not an
accurate depiction of a healthy romantic relationship. Your
mental health matters!

Triggers include: stalking, childhood sexual assault (mentioned),
physical and mental abuse, gore, blood, rape, torture, drug and
alcohol use, crass language, explicit sex, illegal preservation of
organs, and murder.

If you notice something that may have been missed, feel free to
reach out to the author via their website.

For up-to-date trigger lists and more, please visit
HayleyBrianaWrites.com

CHAPTER 1

RAVEN

Another box.

I had hoped that it wouldn't happen again. But that hope was slowly dwindling. Every asshat I'd had issues with in the past had always turned out like this. This time, I was sure it was Travis's heart cast in the resin that sat inside the velvet-lined box.

Honestly, I couldn't care less at this moment. If it really belonged to my cheating ex, good riddance for the female population. The asshole frat boy had been caught cheating on me with some high school girl during one of the house parties. The girl had the nerve to record it and post the shit online. It didn't take long for word to get back to me and the police to get involved.

This would make the third heart to grace my doorstep. The first one being a handsy professor from freshman year. He'd wanted me to improve my grades with *favors* and I'd immediately turned him into the dean. As for the second, it was from the man I'd called my uncle as a child. He'd always had his hands and dick in places they didn't belong when I was too little to understand what was happening. He'd gone to prison when I was ten, but was let out last year on good behavior. Within a week, he'd gone missing, and a heart had ended up on my doorstep. Cased in resin where it lay in a black velvet-lined box, next to a blood red-long stem rose, and tied all pretty with a red silk bow.

I'd had a stalker for as long as I could remember. Since the first time Travis had ever laid his hands on me and I'd ended up in the hospital during my sophomore year. The asshole hadn't even felt sorry. That was probably when I should have known things wouldn't work out with him. But my dumb heart thought that I could change him or make him love me.

But my stalker had never done anything to make me think he was dangerous. I'd catch the red, neon glow of his mask around dark corners from time to time, roses left in places they hadn't been, and hearts left on my doorstep.

Honestly, there could be worse kinds of stalkers.

This one was more like my guardian angel. There to keep an eye on me and to bring swift justice to anyone who did me wrong.

With a sigh, I moved to place the new addition to my growing collection on the mantle of my fireplace. The perfect little trio surrounded by the corpses of all the dying roses left by the mask that lurked in the shadows.

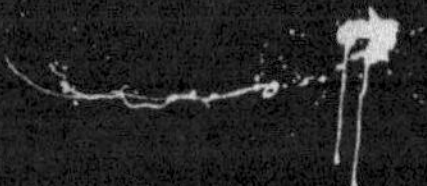

"Again?"

I glance at my father from where I sit, lounging on the opposite side of his desk. He wasn't too happy when I'd sent him a picture of my newest piece of decor this morning.

My father is a very influential man, especially in the dark underground of our *fine* city. Many would say that he runs the mafia, but in reality he's simply a politician who has no problem getting his hands dirty. He's what keeps this city running, while somehow maintaining the perfect image as a politician. That doesn't mean he doesn't sometimes work with the mafia and gangs that run rampant in the streets. It had been the family business for generations. The polished life of a government official, while skeletons were hidden away in closets, or tossed to the bottom of a large body of water.

Real old-timey gangster shit, in my opinion.

"Well, I didn't have three yesterday." I remark, popping my bubble gum loudly. The noise causing my father's eye to twitch in annoyance.

"I will be placing extra security on you for the foreseeable future. I can't have my little girl in danger because of some psychotic stalker."

I roll my eyes, standing to walk around the desk to place a gentle kiss on his forehead.

"It's okay, daddy. I'm positive the guy is harmless. He's been following me around for years now. If he had any intent on hurting me, he would have by now. And I'm not a little girl anymore."

He sighs in frustration. "One bodyguard. That's final, Raven."

I smile, picking up my bag to sling over my shoulder as I make my way towards the door.

"Alight, daddy-o. Just make sure he's cute. You know how much I love to play with them." I grin over my shoulder, quickly slamming the door shut behind me as I hear my father shouting my name.

Too bad I'll be long gone before he makes it through that door.

Sprinting down the hall, I somehow make it to the elevator before it closes. The men and women in suits looking at me as if I've grown three heads as I press the buttons to shut the doors and to head down to the ground floor.

Giving my father a run for his money would always be my favorite pastime.

CHAPTER 2

RAVEN

"You have to go to the Halloween party, Raven. It's supposed to be the biggest one in the fraternity's history. No one is blaming you for the shit that happened with Travis. They haven't even heard from him in two weeks. Not since his daddy paid off that girl's family to make it all go away."

My eyes wandered over to the newest edition of my collection. Its surface shining in the sunlight that filters through the open window. Causing parts of the red vessels to give off a ruby gleam.

"Alright, Ava. I'll go if you really want me to. We will have to go shopping so I can pick out a costume."

"Cool! We can go tonight once I'm finished with my last class." She plops down onto the couch next to me, reaching for the bag of popcorn from the coffee table.

Her eyes tracking over the new heart on my mantle. "I know you're rich and all, but why would you have hearts as decor?"

A snort leaves me as I try not to laugh, taking a bite of popcorn before saying, "They were gifts."

I'd never told her about my stalker, and I didn't think she'd appreciate hearing my theory of where said hearts came from.

No.

That was my own little secret.

"I guess it does fit you, but it's still fucking weird. They look so real it isn't even funny." She toys with a long strand of my midnight black hair as we sit back to finish watching our movie before classes start for the day.

My phone dings, letting me know I've received a text. My father's number flashing on the screen.

A smile gracing my lips as I turned off the phone. He'd taught me at a young age to never take shit from anyone. He just never thought I'd do the same with him. In the end, though, I was set to take over the family business at some point. If I was going to work with and against the baddest of the bad, then I'd do it my way. If they didn't get in line, I knew full well how to put a bullet between their eyes.

CHAPTER 3

HIM

Her body swayed as she walked hand in hand with her little friend. Her ample curves leaving little to the imagination even in her loose fit tee and fitted jeans.

From my time watching my little bird, I'd picked up on all those she spent time with.

This one was named Ava. A bubbly blonde who'd been my little bird's friend since primary school. She was good to my girl, and that was all that mattered.

What I didn't like was the sack of meat that followed them around as they shopped. A new bodyguard. His broad form following after the girls, dressed in all black with a baseball cap on. Their little shadow of protection that also played pack mule. Carrying everything they purchased from the stores they walked out of.

Apparently, daddy dearest wasn't too fond of the newest little gift I'd given his little girl. But she liked it. Like all the others, she placed it in her home like decor. Smiling at them fondly whenever she'd walk past.

Every person who laid a hand on her pretty little head, or hurt her in some way would end up on that mantle.

Until one day, I would make her mine.

That day was coming much sooner than she even realized. The thought causing a grin to spread across my face beneath my hood, before sliding back into the shadows to watch her.

CHAPTER 4

RAVEN

After hours of shopping, I'd finally settled on a dark angel costume. It featured a black mini-skirt, fitted crop top, and black angel wings. I'd pair it with a pair of thigh-high boots and call it a day. The plus side was that the top and skirt could be reused as regular clothes after tonight. If they didn't end up ruined, that is.

Most would say I had no business wearing clothes like this. I wasn't the typical girl who wore such revealing clothes. Not with my curvy frame. But it was what I liked.

After everything that happened in my childhood, I'd put on weight in hopes it would make people like my uncle lose interest. When I'd gotten older, I'd promised myself I'd never let a man decide how I dressed or felt about myself again. While I was considered a mid-sized girl, I worked hard to maintain an hourglass figure and to focus on my health.

I still wasn't looking forward to this party, either.

The parties at the club house always got a bit out of hand. Any alcohol and drug you could think of making its way into the nightly rotation.

Ava had picked a basic playboy bunny outfit. Honestly, it matched her personality and platinum blonde hair to a tee.

My newest bodyguard hauled all our bags into my apartment. Being the perfect little errand boy on our trip out today.

"Ms. Tegan, is there anything else you'll be needing before I take my post?" My new bodyguard said in his deep tenor.

I tossed him a wicked smile. "No, Clint. I'll yell if I need anything."

With a nod of his head and a dusting of pink on his cheeks, he walked out the front door. As soon as said door shut Ava and I burst into laughter.

"God, Raven! Cut the guy some slack." She chastised me through her fit of giggles.

"If you want to take him for a test run, Ava, go for it." I smiled at her knowingly. The two had been fucking each other with their eyes all day.

While I toyed with my father about sleeping with the men he hired or worked with, it wasn't something I was into. With all the shit I'd been through in my life, it was hard to get into the right headspace to be with someone. I always felt dirty afterwards and like I had to be a certain way to make the men in my life happy. Travis had been the only actual boyfriend I'd had since all the fucked up shit. While I could flirt with the best of them, being intimate just wasn't something I was comfortable with. It had been the excuse the asshole had given as to why he'd cheated on me.

"If you aren't going to give me any, I'll find someone who will."

His mocking tone filtered through my mind, causing a pang in my chest. My eyes roaming over his heart that now graced my fireplace mantle.

"We will see what happens," Ava said, pulling me from my thoughts. "I'm going to leave my things here and I'll head over tomorrow night to get ready." She said, prancing over to place a kiss on my cheek before slipping from the apartment.

With an exhausted sigh, I flopped down onto the couch. My eyes finding their way back to my collection of hearts. The thought that my masked stalker would do something for me without asking for anything in return had my stomach fluttering and heat pooling at my core. He was the only one who made me want things I had no business wanting.

"Fuck, Raven. What the hell is wrong with you?" I whispered into the void of my empty apartment.

CHAPTER 5

HIM

She was going out tonight.

I watched through her window as she slipped into the most revealing top and skirt I'd ever seen. My cock aching as I watched her slip into her costume for tonight's party.

Her hair was hanging loose around her in waves. My hand aching to grab it by the handful as I plowed into her. Listening to her moans of pleasure fill her apartment. I bet if I chased her she'd have the prettiest screams of fear too.

The thought had me palming my dick through the fabric of my jeans. I was rock solid just thinking about her, but I had to play my cards right. If I had my way, I would end tonight buried between her thighs.

The amount of times I'd fantasized about her should be alarming. Especially considering the state in which I'd met her. That worthless boyfriend of hers had broken her arm and bloodied her pretty face during a fight two years ago. Saying she'd fallen down a flight of stairs as she held a blood-soaked t-shirt to her face.

At the time, I'd only been there to collect a new corpse to take downstairs to the morgue. But I couldn't help but to watch the broken angel that night. To learn all I could about her in those brief moments. All I needed was her name and address from her files. Then I'd know everything else about her. And for two years I've watched her.

Learned her.

Craved her.

Obsessed over her until she was the only thing that mattered in my world.

I'd gone so far as to begin doing side work for her father. Taking over the job my superior had done for the politician prior to his retirement. It's how I became so good at disposing of bodies and preserving their organs for my little bird. If only he knew his employee was also the man stalking his daughter.

The thought brought a smile to my face underneath the mask I wore. The LEDs turned off, so that I didn't draw too much attention from the shadows. Watching my little bird slip on a set of fishnet thighs through her bedroom window.

Tonight, I would show myself to her.

I would make her mine. Make her beg and crawl to me like my perfect little bird.

She was mine and tonight she'd learn that she would never be rid of me.

CHAPTER 6

RAVEN

Music and smoke filled the small space as we made our way into the frat house. The floors were sticky, sticking to the bottom of my boots as Ava and I slid through all the bodies filling the small entryway.

Somehow I had managed to convince daddy dearest to give my bodyguard the night off somewhat. He'd insisted that he drop us off and had access to track my phone throughout the night, just in case anything happened. But the guy was free to do as he pleased while I was out tonight. Making me promise to call if anything happened.

It was loud as we finally made our way into the kitchen to grab a few glasses of punch before making our way to the dancefloor. My body moved to the beat of the music, the spiked punch already doing a number on my system along with all the flashing lights. Hands grabbed my waist from behind. Not caring about who it could be, I ground my hips back against them. Dancing with anyone and everyone as the night went on.

There was no telling what ended up in the punch tonight as my heart raced and a thin sheen of sweat broke out over my skin. A heat growing in my core.

Shit. The boys had probably slipped ecstasy or something into the punch to improve their chances of getting laid tonight.

I was quickly overheating as I gripped onto Ava's wrist to get her attention. When her eyes found mine, her pupils were blown wide, she'd had far more to drink tonight than me.

"I'll be back." I shouted over the loud music.

She smiled, nodded and went back to dancing with the guy she'd picked out for tonight.

I quickly rushed towards the stairs, knowing that the bathroom on the bottom floor would have a line. I just needed to find an empty bedroom. All the rooms had their own personal bathrooms, and I needed a moment. Just some time to drink some water and calm down from the effects of the alcohol and drugs in my system. Thank god I'd only drank one glass.

Having been involved with someone who had been a part of this fraternity I should have known better than to drink the punch. But I'd wanted to let loose. Everything from the past few years crashing down around me. The heart of my ex showing up on my doorstep. Letting me know he'd never be able to put his hands on me or anyone else again. I hadn't loved him, not truly. Things had been too bad with us to really care that he was gone now.

Finally, I stumbled into an empty room and rushed towards the bathroom. Making it just in time to spill my guts into the toilet as I tried to get everything out.

"Fuck," I groaned as I finally caught my breath, using a wad of tissue to wipe my mouth before getting back to my feet. I was still far too hot as I turned on the cold water to splash my face. Cupping my hands to take a drink of something other than the shit downstairs.

Looking into the mirror I could barely make out the hazel color on my eyes. My pupils were blown, surrounded by my smeared mascara. The black matching that of the wings currently strapped to my back. I really looked a mess. But that burning ache between my legs just wouldn't go away. I needed to take care of that before I ended up in bed with some asshole tonight.

Drying my face, using a hand towel from a cabinet to clean up some of the mascara from around my eyes. With a sigh, I made my way back into the connecting bedroom, locked the door and pressed my heated forehead to the doorframe.

"Best to get it over with," I mumbled turning to face the room.

My breath caught in my lungs as a glowing mask stared back at me from the desk chair in the corner. It's red-X eyes watching me as a gloved hand flipped a switch blade.

"You." I sounded breathless as I stood there, staring at the man who'd been my shadow for the past two years.

My core seemed to go into overdrive at the realization that he was here in the room with me. I was sure at this point that my desire was leaking down my thighs, making everything slick beneath my skirt.

My masked man said nothing, simply used his knife to point towards the empty bed.

The fact he thought he could just boss me around had anger filling my head. At my core I could be a brat and wasn't the most fond of being told what to do.

If this guy thought he could scare me into doing what he wanted, he was dead wrong. If he was going to watch me, then I'd give him a show he'd never fucking forget.

I smirked at him, stalking directly towards where he sat rather than the bed where he pointed. Dropping to my knees in front of him as I trailed my hands up his black jean clad thighs. If the muscles I felt through the material were any indication, he was built. The thought that he could crush my head like a watermelon like the guys online did had a fresh wave of desire rushing through me. I'd always thought the idea of my stalker was hot. Using the glances I'd gotten of him as my personal spank-bank.

"You've been watching me," I said. Slipping my hands higher until I could feel his hard length beneath my palm.

"You leave me gifts," I continued, unbuttoning his jeans until his enormous cock sprang free. My mouth watered at the sight. It was massive. The kind of cock made for film with its swollen head and the veins that traced down the length. There was a bead of pre-cum at the tip, and I didn't fight the urge to taste. Taking the head into my mouth as his salty flavor exploded on my tongue. My eyes never leaving the glowing Xs that watched my every move. A groan of pleasure came from inside the mask as I took him further into my mouth, sucking him, coaxing more of his flavor onto my tongue.

I'd never been a fan of blow jobs, but for my stalker I could make an exception. He was far too big to completely fit in my mouth, so I moved a hand to wrap around the base of his dick. Using it as extra leverage as I bobbed on his length. The head knocked into the back of my throat until I couldn't breathe on each downward stroke.

It didn't take him long to get into it either. His free hand that wasn't holding the knife fisted into my hair where he forced me further down his length until he was fucking up into me. I gagged around his cock, tears streaming down my face as I tried to catch my breath every time he pulled me up before thrusting deep again.

My clit throbbed as he used me for his own pleasure. The glowing eyes and smile of his mask shooting spikes of fear into me as I watched him unravel.

Warning bells blared in my head. Telling me that I had no business in a room with my stalker, let alone having his dick shoved down my throat.

Instead of listening to that little voice in my head I hollowed out my cheeks, sucking on the throbbing cock in my mouth until I could feel it pulse. Against all reason I wanted to taste him. I wanted him to brand me with his come, just to show my appreciation for the gifts he left for me.

A growl reverberated from behind the mask as he pulled me off by my hair, an audible pop filling the room as he pulled me off his dick. Before I even knew what was happening I was face down on the mattress with my ass in the air. The hand in my hair pressing my face into the blankets as the mask fell to the bed next to me.

He was holding me in place so that I couldn't see him as cool steel slid up the inside of my thigh to my core. I didn't even breathe as I felt the blade slide under the fabric of my thong before feeling a tug and a snap as the material was cut from my core. Leaving me completely exposed to my stalker.

Before the panic of what was happening could set in, the knife fell to the bed next to me. A moan fell from my lips as he took his cock in his hand to drag the head from my clit to my ass. Spreading my desire over his length and my folds. Every stroke against my throbbing clit bringing me higher and higher as pleasure coursed through me.

"Please," I begged, needing something to relieve the ache and fire that was consuming me. I knew it was whatever had been in the drink making me so bold, but I wanted him.

It didn't take much begging though as he pressed the head of his cock against my entrance and slammed inside.

A scream of pain shredding its way up my throat at the intrusion. But he didn't stop. Didn't give my body a moment to process what was happening as he fucked me like his own personal sex toy. The only relief being that I was so fucking wet from the drugs in my system.

His hand reached around, finding my clit as he pounded into me. Drawing his fingers in the most tantalizing circles until I was seeing stars and thrusting my hips back to meet every one of his thrusts.

The hand in my hair loosened as he reached down to grab his mask. I was so blissed out I couldn't even turn my head to catch a glimpse of my stalker.

I wanted to know what he looked like under the mask. I wanted him more than I'd ever wanted anything in my life. It was as if I was lost in a desert landscape and he was the only drink of water.

With one final thrust, I came. Screaming out in pleasure as my core clamped around his cock. My fluids leaked down my thighs as he continued to thrust into me. Drawing out the orgasm until I was whimpering and clawing at the sheets.

As the waves of pleasure began to fade he pulled out, leaving an ache from the stretch in his wake.

"I'm not finished with you yet, little bird." He growled in a deep timber.

CHAPTER 7

HIM

Her breath seemed to halt in her chest as I turned her onto her back. Her pretty black wings fanned out around her. Making her look as if she were a fallen angel at my mercy.

I'd put the mask back in place to hide who I was. It wasn't the right time for her to know who had been watching her from the shadows.

No.

Tonight was all about giving into the desires I'd felt for her over the years of watching her.

I knew she wasn't in her right mind, if her eyes and flushed skin after one drink was any indication. But I couldn't help myself. She was so willing. I'd only intended on watching her bring herself to pleasure tonight. But the moment her red painted lips wrapped around my cock I knew I was done for. I wouldn't stop until I was filling her tight cunt as she came for me. Milking me dry.

Her legs spread wide for me, giving me the perfect view of her glistening pink pussy. My mouth watered for a taste, but that would have to wait for now. She deserved to be worshiped like the goddess she was.

I took her hands in mine, pulling them to rest above her head as I fitted myself between her thighs. Her heels locking into place around my waist as I slammed back into her waiting cunt.

Her back arched off the bed as she made the prettiest little mewls of pleasure. Every pulse of her pussy around me drew me closer to my own release, but I wanted more of her.

Needed more of her.

I could die with this perfect hole strangling my cock.

My hands moved to roam over her perfect body. Over the generous curves of her breasts. Feeling the hardened peaks through the thin fabric of her shirt. Pinching her nipples until her moans of pleasure turned to whimpers. With every thrust and pinch, the walls of her pussy clamped down around my dick.

"Does my little bird like a little pain with her pleasure?" My voice rasped, distorted by the mask I wore.

Her moan of pleasure was the only response she gave. She hadn't even seemed to realize that I was no longer holding her wrists as my hands wondered. Fingers moving to pinch at her swollen clit as I fucked her tight little hole.

"Use your words, little bird." I rasped. Balls drawing tights as I came closer to my own release.

"Yes!" She screamed out, her pussy convulsing around my dick as she came, soaking the bed underneath her. Her nails digging into my forearms as she reached for something to hold on to as she rode out the waves of her pleasure.

Soon I was following her right over the edge, my cock throbbing as I came inside her welcoming cunt. Continuing to thrust and work her clit with my fingers to prolong her orgasm until she was gasping and whimpering underneath me.

With one final thrust I pulled out, readjusting myself back into my jeans before pulling the mask away from my face to get some air flow without showing her my face just yet.

Damn, this thing was hot. The heat from my breathing causing condensation to gather inside the mask. After tonight, hopefully I wouldn't need the thing anymore.

Raven lay there, tangled in the sheets, gasping for breath as she stared at the ceiling in complete bliss. Her legs still spread wide where I could see the combination of us both leaking from her thoroughly used hole. With a grin, I moved my fingers down to her core. Gathering up the liquid to push back into her. The intrusion causing her walls to clamp down around my gloved fingers.

"Such a greedy cunt."

Good.

Tonight would be a night for us both to remember.

CHAPTER 8

RAVEN

Holy fucking hell.

I couldn't seem to get my mind right after the best orgasm of my life. My heart raced as I watched the masked man gather the come between my legs and push it back into me. If I hadn't been on the pill, I probably would have been in a panic about all this.

A moan slipping free at just how dirty this all was. His words only making his actions hotter. I'd just let a complete stranger in a mask, who'd been stalking me, fuck my brains out. I couldn't even find the give a fuck to care.

I was still fucked up from the alcohol and drugs, but I felt better than I had in a very long time as I sat up in the bed. Watching as the masked man took off his gloves and the hoodie he'd been wearing. Leaving him in his dark jeans and a fitted black t-shirt. The shorter sleeves giving me the perfect view of the tattoos that covered his arms, hands, and neck.

My mouth watered at the sight as his muscles flexed as he moved around the room.

Before I could lose my nerve, I pulled the remains of my panties down my legs. Balling the lace in my hand as I stood on shaking legs to walk directly towards him. Slipping the torn material into the front pocket of his jeans.

"Just a little trophy." I teased, before slipping out the room.

If he wanted more from me he knew where to find me.

The party was still in full swing as I made my way back downstairs. Swiping an unopened beer from the cooler. I'd learned my lesson about having something out in the open.

Finding Ava still dancing in the crowd, a full glass of punch in her hand, I grabbed another beer before making my way over.

"Hey!" She turned to yell at me as I took the cup from her hand, not giving a shit as I tossed it into the nearest trash can.

"They put something in the punch." I said, placing the unopened beer in her hand.

She smiled, placing a quick kiss on my lips before turning back to her dance partner of the night.

With a shake of my head, I moved through the crowd, waiting for my masked man to find me again. His come leaking down my legs until I was nearly panting with need all over again.

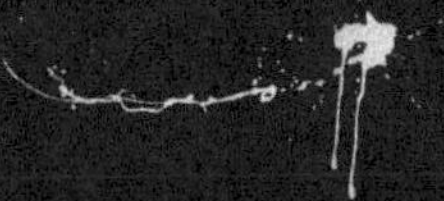

It didn't take long for him to find me. His hands gripped onto my waist as we began to dance in the crowd. The glow of his mask giving me a sense of safety as he pulled me close.

"Will you ever take it off?" I asked, toying with the wicked smile of the mask.

"If you're sure, little bird." He seemed to purr as his hands gripped my ass, pulling me flush against his hard body.

Fuck, this guy worked out, a lot. I bet he could fuck me against a wall with ease. I'd have to mention it at some point, but right now I was dying to see what he hid under the mask. It was like opening a present on Christmas morning, but better.

Taking a deep breath, I pulled the mask from his face, giving me the perfect view of the man who'd been my shadow. His dark hair was tousled from the mask, giving him the perfect, not so put together look. His features were sharp, giving way to the short beard he had, a silver lip ring shining in the corner of his lip. But most of all, I took in the haunting green eyes that took in my every movement. He was by far the most attractive man I'd ever laid eyes on.

While the mask had been hot, he had a face I just wanted to sit on. My core aching at the thought.

"If you keep fucking me with your eyes, I'll have to bend you over and fuck that pretty pussy right here in front of everyone." He growled, eyes shining with the dare he'd just thrown at me.

"I'd much rather ride your face." I blurted, flashing him my most flirtatious smile. I wasn't shy, and I'd never pretend to be either.

With a move so quick I couldn't even protest, he had me up in the air, my legs around his waist. His hands supporting me by my ass as he pressed me into the nearest wall. The hard bulge in his jeans pressing perfectly against my core. He ground into me until I was sure I'd soaked through his jeans.

I was shocked that he'd lifted me with such ease. Not even struggling or grunting as he held me in place.

"Play nice," He said, just before his mouth found mine. Forcing his tongue into my mouth in a hot, sloppy kiss where we fought for dominance. Even though I knew I'd never win against him, I wanted to rile him up. Wanted to drive him the best sort of crazy until he bent me over his knee and spanked me.

The kiss ended far too soon as he sat me on my feet, pulling me back towards the dance floor.

"What can I even call you?" I asked as I draped my arms over his shoulders while dancing. From this position, it was clear he was much taller than my 5'2" frame. He had to be at least six feet tall.

"Voss," was his only response as he ground against me. The dance turning more into something like from *Dirty Dancing*.

It was as if he were just getting started on all the things he wanted to do tonight. Honestly, I'd follow this man to hell and back just for another taste.

CHAPTER 9

VOSS

By the time the party was winding down, my cock was as hard as steel. All the dancing and teasing with my girl tonight had me ready for another taste of her.

"I have to find my friend. Once I know she's home safe, maybe you could come over to my place?" She said as we stepped over all the passed out bodies that surrounded us. She'd discarded her wings sometime in the night, placing my mask on her head like some sort of hat.

I didn't answer her. If she thought she would get rid of me that easily, she had no idea how obsessed I was.

"She's not down here." She pouted, turning to head upstairs.

It didn't take long to find her friend, but not in a way my little bird had hoped. She was passed out in a bed, with some asshole and his two friends standing around taking turns on her unconscious body. Frat boys really pissed me off. Every single one was a predator.

"What the hell," Raven shouted, grabbing the attention of the guys in the room.

With my hand on her back I maneuvered her further into the room, shutting and locking the door behind us. Not one of these assholes was getting out of here tonight.

Sensing the danger, the guy who'd been between Ava's legs moved to tuck himself away.

"Oh, you brought us another one buddy?" He said, moving to pat me on the shoulder as if we were good friends. He didn't make it far though before my hand was wrapped around his throat and I was smashing his face into the bedside table.

Over and over again, I slammed his face into the wood until the place was covered in blood and the guy was knocked the fuck out. I wasn't even sure he was still alive when I dropped him to the floor.

"What the fuck, man?" One of his friends asked, trying to get past me to the door.

"I don't much care for assholes that force themselves on women." Was all I said before throwing a fist into the guy's face that tried to run past. His fists went flying in an attempt to fight me off as he screamed for his buddy to run for help. A smile twisting my lips when I realized these two would put up a fight.

"Don't let the other one get out, little bird." I said, nodding towards an aluminum baseball bat in the corner before driving my fist into the face of the one I had just pinned to the floor.

A wicked smile spread across her ruby lips as she pulled my mask down over her face and reached for the bat. That sight alone had me ready to be buried balls deep in her again.

My little bird might just be as fucked up as I was.

CHAPTER 10

RAVEN

The bat fit snugly in my hands as the guy basically pissed himself as I stood between him and the door.

To think he was about to rape my best friend and now there was a growing wet spot in the front of his jeans when a girl in a mask stood between him and freedom. The thought had a chuckle wanting to burst from me.

The boys in the frat house really were a piece of work. Spoiled little rich kids with daddy's money and no balls to back up their shit. At least I had no problem getting my hands dirty. My daddy had taught me well.

"Awww, poor little baby getting scared?" I teased, swinging the bat around and around.

A gurgling sound filled the room, causing me to turn to see Voss slide his blade across the other guy's throat.

Pissy boy must have thought that was his chance as he lunged forward. Probably hoping to knock me out of the way to make it through the door.

But I was faster. Side stepping at the same time as I swung the bat. The metal collided with his kneecaps before he could ever reach for the handle. The sickening crunch of bones filled the silence as he fell to the floor, screaming and clutching at his now busted knees as tears streamed down his face.

I tsked at him, circling him while dragging the bat across the floor. The sound just seemed to make him sob harder. He'd already pissed himself, what else could I do other than put him out of his misery.

"Did you already get your turn with her?" I asked, pressing the bat into his broken knee.

"No!" He screamed, snot and tears coating his face. He really was pathetic.

"Then, I guess I'll make this quick for you." I said swinging the bat high and into the back of his head. Repeating the move until there was only a lump of flesh and blood left where his head had once been.

"Damn, little bird." Voss chuckled, coming behind me to wrap his muscular arms around my waist. I could feel his hardened length pressing into me and it sent a moan from my lips.

Lips trailed up my neck, nipping at the tender flesh. His hands skating down my now blood covered stomach until he was bunching my skirt around my waist. Fingers wasting no time in delving into my aching core. Curling deep inside until I was seeing stars as he worked me.

"We can't. I have to take Ava to be seen. Make sure she's alright." I gasped out, fighting the building pleasure.

His teeth bit into my earlobe before he removed his fingers. A whimper leaving me at the loss.

"My truck is parked down the street. I'll drive us to the hospital. I have to take these assholes to the morgue and I'm positive the first guy is just knocked out. I'll let you take care of him once you've got your friend taken care of." He placed a gentle kiss on my cheek before moving to clean up the dead assholes. In confirmation, the first guy groaned.

Oh, I'd have fun making him pay for what he did to Ava.

Without thinking, I swung the bat, knocking him out cold once more. We didn't need him waking up before we were ready for him.

I was covered in blood, but I knew I could spin a convincing story about a crazy guy showing up at the party and causing a scene.

"Voss, on second thought, just grab their hearts. I want you to show me how you preserve them. Leave the bodies here and take this one. Make it look like some psycho showed up. I'll give my dad a call. He'll have his guys set the scene like some break in gone wrong and pin it on someone the cops can focus on."

He actually laughed, "Damn, little bird. When you talk like that, it makes me want to bend you over and fuck that pretty pussy of yours."

I smiled, moving to get my best friend out of this hellhole. "Time for that later."

CHAPTER 11

RAVEN

Voss had slipped through a back entrance after dropping me and Ava at the front of the emergency room.

The place had been in an uproar as they ushered us into a room. Ava had woken just a bit on the way to the hospital and was still out of it as she was examined. I held her hand through it all. Reassuring the nurses that I was completely fine, and the blood was from falling on the dead bodies when I went looking for my friend.

I'd called daddy on the way here. He was already spinning a story about how gang violence was responsible for the night's events. His crew making it back to the house to clean up any sign of our involvement before authorities arrived on scene.

He hadn't been happy about me connecting with my stalker, but hell, he'd get over it. Apparently Voss was in his employ as well. It explained the whole morgue thing, at least. Voss was one of his cleaners who made people disappear. It was also how he knew so much about organ preservation.

What I didn't expect was for him to show up with his tattoos on display in a set of black scrubs and freshly showered. His demeanor had completely changed as he spoke with nurses as if they were good friends. That is until his eyes landed on me. He made a show of seeming concerned. Rushing from the nurse he'd been speaking to towards the room where we waited. When no one else was looking, I caught the flicker of heat in his eyes before he pulled me from my seat and into his arms.

"Play along," he whispered in my ear before pulling me away from me, hands holding onto my shoulders as he looked me over.

"What the hell, baby? Why didn't you tell me you were one of the ones brought in from that mess tonight?" He genuinely seemed worried as he pushed the hair away from my face, frantically searching for any wounds I may have had.

"It's not my blood. I'm fine, but Ava was in bad shape." I said as he pulled me from the room. A nurse who'd been working on Ava rushed over.

"You didn't tell me you were the girl Dr. Kieran's been gushing over." She said, handing me a cup of coffee.

"It slipped my mind," I said, looking back towards Ava's closed door. "I was so focused on Ava that I wasn't worried about anything else."

Voss, Dr. Kieran, wrapped his arm around my shoulders to pull me close. "I'm going to take her downstairs to get her cleaned up. If anything happens with Ava, please page me."

The nurse nodded before going back to work.

Voss led me down the hall and to an elevator that took us down to the basement. I assumed the morgue was located down there. As soon as the door to the elevator closed, I looked him over with confusion. He just smirked, holding a finger to his lips in a *shushing* motion. So, I bit my tongue as we rode the elevator down and he led me into the freezing cold morgue.

"It's fucking freezing in here." I shivered, wrapping my arms around my torso for warmth.

"Once we are finished with our little friend, I'll help you into a warm shower and clean clothes." His breath brushed over my ear as he whispered. Large hands rubbing along my arms.

At the reminder, my eyes scanned the room, landing on the man strapped to the table. He was gagged, eyes pried open with the craziest tools I'd ever seen. Tears leaked down his temples as he fought to free himself from the restraints that held him in place.

"I wanted to make sure he saw everything you planned to do to him." My shadow's voice had taken on a dark edge. No longer playing at being the worried boyfriend from upstairs.

"Sounds good to me, *Dr. Kieran.*" I emphasized his name as I stepped away from him. Walking over to a table with an array of tools scattered about. My fingers brushing over the cold metal.

"Is it possible to remove someone's heart while they are still alive?" I found myself asking, picking up a surgical blade to twist between my fingers. The light shone off the blade as it slowly spun.

CHAPTER 12

VOSS

I hadn't been expecting her question as I watched her examine the tools of my trade.

"Yes. At least until the blood flow to the organ is cut off, and it is removed." I answered, wondering exactly what my little bird had in mind.

That wicked smile lit up her face as she laid down the scalpel and went back to browsing. "Can you tell me what I'll need to do everything?"

"First, I'll need to paralyze him. Administer specific drugs to keep him awake, but make sure he can't move." I pointed out each tool she'd need as I explained the steps. "You'll need to cut through his skin and muscles in a y-shape across his chest and stomach. Once you have him open, you'll take these rib spreaders to crack open his ribs. This will give you access to his heart, lungs, and other organs."

She was completely engrossed in every tool I pointed out as I continued to explain the process.

How she'd clamp off specific areas of the heart to stop the blood flow before cutting through each vessel and valve. That at this point, his organs would begin to shut down from lack of blood flow, until he was dead. How I could then help her place the severed heart on ice to begin the process of preserving it along with the other two.

My girl would have a collection of hearts, and I couldn't wait to help her collect each one.

She smiled over her shoulder at me, a twinkle in her eye as she said, "can you get it all ready for me?"

"Anything for you, little bird." I said, pulling her close and kissing her. A fire ignited in my chest at the brief contact before I got to work.

CHAPTER 13

RAVEN

Voss got to work administering all sorts of drugs I couldn't name. He'd placed an IV with skill and quickly got to work setting everything up for me. He stood the table up at an angle so that it was easier for me to reach. Cutting off the frat boy's clothes for easier access.

Said frat boy was a whimpering mess. His eyes still pried open with the speculums, as the beautiful doctor before me had explained.

"So, if you're an actual doctor, why do you work in the morgue?" I asked, sitting on top of the counter with my legs swinging back and forth. Excitement dancing in my blood for what was about to happen.

"During my residency, I was assigned to learn from the medical examiner. I found it more rewarding with less patient interaction. So my superior took me under his wing, and I took over once he retired. That's how I started working for your father as well." He stated it as if it were a matter of fact. Like it explained everything as he pressed the plunger on the final medication into the IV.

Once he was finished with the drugs, he took a sharpie and began mapping out the places I would cut soon. My fingers itched to get started before the drugs took effect. But I wanted him awake for everything I did to him.

He'd hurt my friend. He was the reason she had been upstairs crying. The reason she had to go through the embarrassment of being checked for any possible STDs those assholes had.

No, he wouldn't walk out of this room tonight. His heart would be my newest piece that graced my mantle.

He would never hurt anyone else again.

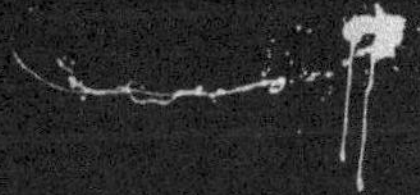

"Are you certain you want to be the one to do this?" Voss asked as he moved the tools onto a stand next to the table.

I nodded, moving to stand beside him, taking a scalpel in my hand. You'd think I would be shaking like a leaf, but my hands were steady as I looked between the naked man in front of me and the sharp blade.

"Will he bleed out if I cut his worthless cock off first?" The question caused him to whimper behind the gag, a smile spreading over my face once more. This was going to be fun.

"It's very unlikely." Voss said, leaning against the counter with his arms crossed. His tattoos flexing under the toned muscles of his forearms.

"You're very distracting." I smirked at him, taking a moment to check out my once stalker. Fuck, he was a god. One I wanted to worship until I could no longer feel my legs.

Maybe after all this was over.

With that final thought, I got to work.

"You know, you'd think considering you like to drug and rape women you'd at least have a big dick." I spoke while I lifted his tiny cock with the blade of the scalpel, not caring if it was already cutting into him. "Sadly, this might be the smallest one I've ever seen."

The blade cut through the skin and muscle like butter. A few swipes, and the thing was dropping to the floor. Tears streamed down his face as he watched every single thing I did to him. Feeling the pain but unable to do more than whimper and cry.

"Did it make you feel powerful? Like some sort of fucked up god when you fucked women who wouldn't have wanted you to begin with?" The line of questioning went on and on. The drugs making it impossible for him to scream or answer. He was still gagged though, and I wasn't entirely sure what the drugs did to him. So maybe he could have answered. I wasn't willing to remove the gag to find out.

My heart still raced at the thought that anyone from upstairs could come down here to find us in this situation. The slight panic only fueling the adrenaline flowing through my system.

His cries and whimpers were the only sounds as my blade cut through the y-shaped lines Voss had drawn for me. My hands were slick from the blood, but I was too engrossed in what I was doing to even care.

Blood soaked the floor already from his severed cock and the skin I currently cut through. Soaking into the velvet material of my boots. Oh well, I could always buy a new pair after all this.

When it came time to use the rib spreader, Voss moved closer to me. My back to his front as we both forced the tool to rip open the asshole's ribcage.

The guy's eyes rolled into the back of his head from the pain. Something Voss gave him, making it impossible for him to pass out from the pain.

"Wakey, wakey," I taunted, slapping his tear-stained face. Blood from my hand smearing across his skin that was becoming pale from the blood loss. His eyes finding mine once more as I reached into his chest, feeling his heart beating in the palm of my hand.

"It really is a shame you can't see this. The way your heart pumps blood through your worthless body while I hold it in my hand."

I watched as Voss went to work clamping off the different vessels until the heart's beats became uneven. Gasps and groans of pain the only sounds from the douchebag alongside the squelching of blood.

The heart went wild in my hands as the organ rushed to try to save its host. Unable to do its job his body began to shut down.

"Sad, this couldn't have lasted longer." I whispered, turning my knife to cut through the arteries and veins that held the heart in place.

It wasn't long before he'd stopped breathing, and the blood that had once gushed simply dripped. Like the slow drip of a leaky faucet. Soon, the weight of a heart sat heavy in my hand, completely cut from the body of this asshole.

I was starting to crash. All the excitement of the night fading away until I felt nearly nothing. I watched as Voss took the heart, moving to start the preservation process.

"How exactly does it work?" I asked, moving to watch him work over his shoulder.

He said nothing, simply handing me a mask before putting on his own and a pair of sterile gloves.

I wasn't even sure he'd answer me until he began to speak. "It's called plastination. It will take some time to get through the entire process. First, I'll start an embalming process. Then once that's complete all bodily fluids and fats must be replaced with acetone, then that is replaced with plastic polymers. Once everything is set, it can be preserved in resin. Much like the ones that grace your mantle."

I was entranced as I watched him work and explain the process. I still didn't understand it, but it soon became apparent that he'd become very skilled in his preservation work.

"There is a shower and change of clothes in that back room. Get yourself cleaned up while I take care of our mess." He turned placing a gentle kiss on my lips and pointing me toward his small bathroom. A set of scrubs that were far too big for me folded neatly on the counter.

I still felt numb. All the joy I'd felt earlier drained away as I stood under the scalding water from the showerhead. Watching as the blood and water went down the drain. I wasn't sure how long I stood there, but nearly jumped out of my skin when hands wrapped around me from behind.

"It's just me, little bird." Voss whispered in my ear, before placing gentle kisses along my neck. I leaned back into him, a soft sigh leaving me as I felt all his hard muscles pressed against my bare skin.

He began washing me. Taking his time to glide a soapy rag over my skin to wash away all the blood from the night. Massaging my scalp as he washed my hair. Hand working out any stiff muscles he found until I was nearly dead on my feet.

When he was done, I sat on the shower bench and watched him wash himself. Taking in how his defined muscles flexed and how his prominent veins bulged from his brawny forearms. His fingers and hands working with a skill and grace I'd never seen before.

What was it about forearms and hands that got me all sorts of hot and bothered. A throbbing of my core causing me to shift uncomfortably. Pressing my thighs together did not help to give me the friction I needed. That I craved.

When he turned to rinse off, I gasped as how hard his cock was. Standing proud, with a slight curve. The head deeper in color from the strain as blood rushed to the member.

It was a nice fucking cock, and my mouth watered for another taste.

The clearing of his throat broke me from my staring as my eyes shot up to his. A gleam in their green depths as he grinned down at me.

CHAPTER 14

RAVEN

"Keep looking at me like that, and I'll have to eat you, little bird." His eyes darkened as he looked me over.

The look he gave me sent shivers up my spine. I could feel the heat and pulsing of my core as desire flooded my system. Chancing away the numb feeling I'd had before.

"Then do it." I taunted, leaning my back against the cold tiles of the shower and spreading my legs wide. Showing him just how slick I was as I slid a finger through my glistening folds.

A primal growl seemed to rumble in his chest as he watched me play with myself. Sliding a finger inside to stroke my g-spot, causing a low moan to leave me.

My eyes closed in pleasure as I worked that sweet spot, the palm of my hand giving just the smallest amount of friction to my clit.

I should have been paying attention, because I didn't even noticed he'd moved closer until his hands were wrapping around my thighs and I was being lifted from the bench. My back pressed hard against the tiles as he positioned me on his shoulders. The movement causing me to remove my hand from my throbbing pussy to grip onto his hair. His mouth finding my core as he devoured me.

"Voss," I moaned as his tongue slid into me. "I'm too heavy."

He bit my clit lightly, causing me to gasp. "You're not heavy, little bird. Now shut up and drown me with this sweet cunt."

He wasted no time diving back in, sucking my clit into his mouth before sliding his tongue deep. His movement precise as I threw my head back, eyes rolling as the tension in my belly tightened, winding up like a spring that was ready to snap.

One hand snaked around my thigh, fingers moving to plunge into my pussy as his mouth worked my clit. Groans on pleasure vibrating against my core as he feasted on me. His arms were the only thing holding me up as he ate me against the wall. My hands fisting his hair for purchase as he brought me closer and closer to an orgasm I knew would ruin me.

"Oh fuck. Voss, I can't." I moaned, feeling the pleasure building. My hips rocking against his face.

"That's it baby, ride my face." He growled against my heated skin before diving back in. His muscular arms wrapped tighter around me to hold me in place as his tongue and fingers worked me.

My eyes rolled back as I arched into him. Pleasure exploding like a bomb as I came harder than I ever had in my life. My screams of pleasure filled the bathroom, amplified by the small space.

He didn't stop until the pulsing of my core faded and I was boneless against the wall.

His chuckle causing me to finally open my eyes as he slid me from his shoulders. His arms still wrapped around me as my legs wound around his waist. He was still rock hard as his cock slid against my sensitive pussy. My release shining on his lips as he claimed my mouth. Allowing my taste to coat my tongue as he took control. It was depraved, but the hunger in his kiss caused me to moan, sucking my flavor from his tongue.

"I'm not nearly finished with you yet," He whispered against my lips before slamming his cock home in one fluid thrust of his hips.

My nails dug into his shoulders as my back arched at the intrusion. Pain and pleasure warring inside of me in a heady mix as he fucked me roughly.

This man would be the death of me.

EPILOGUE

RAVEN

"After the massacre that occurred last Halloween, authorities are advising party goers to be on the lookout. The suspect is still on the loose. Over the past two weeks, three additional bodies have been found with their hearts missing…"

The news went on to explain about the *Shattered Heart Killer* who'd been going after pretty rich boys who'd gotten away with raping girls. I smiled at the screen, my eyes trailing over to the bookshelf that now houses nine hearts encased in resin.

More to be added soon.

We'd been working hard to find the candidates for this year, and Voss was busy at work preparing for everything we would need. I, however, was at home, having just finished getting ready and drinking a glass of bubbly white wine.

"Shattered Hearts Killler? That's the best they could come up with?" A deep voice that sent shivers up my spine said from behind me.

"They really aren't that original." I smiled, taking another sip of my drink. Strong hands moved to my shoulders before something was draped around my neck.

Looking down, a necklace sat, its silver and red colors glimmering in the low lighting of my living room. My fingers reached for the heart-shaped pendant, admiring its beauty as Voss placed a gentle kiss on my hair. It was the perfect sort of gift to match all the hearts he'd given me, including his own.

"Happy anniversary, little bird." He whispers, slipping my mask over my face. The pink glow of the LED Xs turning my vision rosy.

Time for another fun Halloween night.

ALSO BY HAYLEY BRIANA

The Hellfire Series

Angel of Blood

Angel in Chains

Sweetest of Fires

Hellfire

Fires of Damnation

Hellfire & Ash: Omnibus Collection Edition (coming soon)

My Bloody Valentine (coming soon)

Darkside Fairytales Series

Belong to Me

All Mad (coming soon)

Be My Guest (coming soon)

On the Hook (coming soon)

Heart of Thieves (coming soon)

Wilted Rose (coming soon)

As White as Snow (coming soon)

Haunting Series

My Dark Haunting

My Dark Terror

My Dark Dolly

My Dark Ending

Haunting: The Series Collection

The Fall Series

Fall From Grace

Fall to Sin (coming soon)

ABOUT THE AUTHOR

Hayley Briana is from a small southern town and from a multi-racial family. She currently resides in Colorado along with her husband, daughter, and fur babies. As a mom & wife, she finds herself in need of some major self-care in the form of a good cup of coffee (or wine/vodka) and a good book. Escaping into a world of fantasy is Hayley's favorite pass time outside of her day-to-day responsibilities. When she's not adulting or writing, you can most likely find her tucked away in her home-library.

For more info on Hayley and what she is working on, please visit HayleyBrianaWrites.com.

Follow Hayley on Social

Instagram.com/hbrianawrites

TikTok.com/@beautyandthebookcase

www.ingramcontent.com/pod-product-compliance
Lightning Source LLC
Chambersburg PA
CBHW040132150726
48005CB00015B/2471